To my beloved son Sean

WE BOTH READ®

Parent's Introduction

We Both Read is the first series of books designed to invite parents and children to share the reading of a story by taking turns reading aloud. This "shared reading" innovation, which was developed in conjunction with early reading specialists, invites parents to read the more sophisticated text on the left-hand pages, while children are encouraged to read the right-hand pages, which have been written at one of three early reading levels.

Reading aloud is one of the most important activities parents can share with their child to assist their reading development. However, *We Both Read* goes beyond reading *to* a child and allows parents to share reading *with* a child. *We Both Read* is so powerful and effective because it combines two key elements in learning: "showing" (the parent reads) and "doing" (the child reads). The result is not only faster reading development for the child, but a much more enjoyable and enriching experience for both!

Most of the words used in the child's text should be familiar to them. Others can easily be sounded out. An occasional difficult word will be first introduced in the parent's text, distinguished with **bold lettering**. Pointing out these words, as you read them, will help familiarize them to your child. You may also find it helpful to read the entire book aloud yourself the first time, then invite your child to participate on the second reading. Also note that the parent's text is preceded by a "talking parent" icon: ☜ ; and the child's text is preceded by a "talking child" icon: ☞ .

We Both Read books is a fun, easy way to encourage and help your child to read — and a wonderful way to start your child off on a lifetime of reading enjoyment!

We Both Read: The Perfect Gift (El Regalo Perfecto)

We Both Read™ is a trademark of Treasure Bay, Inc.

Published by Treasure Bay, Inc.
17 Parkgrove Drive
South San Francisco, CA 94080 USA

PRINTED IN SINGAPORE

Library of Congress Catalog Number: 2001 131597

141-1119

Hardcover ISBN 1-891327-33-X
Paperback ISBN 1-891327-34-8

FIRST EDITION

We Both Read™ Books
Patent No. 5,957,693

WE BOTH READ®

The Perfect Gift

By Jenny Gago

Illustrated by Laurie Harden

TREASURE BAY

Mama was reaching high to water her **pretty** plant when she heard giggles behind her. She turned to find my sister Maria and my cousin Carlos smiling up at her.

*Mamá estaba echando agua a su planta **bonita** cuando escucho risa atras de ella. Dio la vuelta y encontro a mi hermana Maria y a mi primo Carlos sonriendose a ella.*

"That is a **pretty** plant, Mama," Maria said.

Carlos said it was pretty, too. Then they ran off to Maria's room.

*"Esa es una planta **bonita**, Mamá," dijo Maria.*

Carlos dijo que tambien era bonita, y se fueron corriendo al cuarto de Maria.

Grandma looked up from her book and raised her eyebrows. "I think they're up to something, Rosa."

Then she turned to me and said, "Why don't you follow them, Ricky, and see what they're **planning**?"

Abuelita alsó la mirada de su libro y levantó sus cejas. "Yo creo que estan haciendo algo, Rosa."

*Después se dio vuelta y me dijo, "Porque no los sigues, Ricky, y ve que estan **planeando**?"*

I went to Maria's room.
I asked them what they were **planning**.

Fui al cuarto de Maria.
Les pregunté si ***planeaban*** *algo.*

Maria and cousin Carlos said they were planning to buy Mama the perfect present for her birthday tomorrow.

They showed me ten shiny coins they had saved and asked me to walk them to **Mr. Garcia's market**.

Maria y Carlos me dijeron que estaban planeando comprarle a Mamá el regalo perfecto para su cumpleaños.

*Me enseñaron diez monedas brillantes que habian juntado y me pidieron que los acompañe **al mercado del Señor Garcia.***

I took them to **Mr. Garcia's market**.
Mr. Garcia smiled and asked us to come in.

*Fuimos **al mercado del Señor Garcia**.*
Señor Garcia sonrio y nos pidio que pasemos.

Maria and Carlos ran eagerly into the store. They looked up and down every aisle and saw lots of nice things, but nothing that was **perfect**.

*Maria y Carlos entraron a la tienda con entusiasmo. Miraron para arriba y para abajo en cada fila y vieron muchas cosas bonitas, pero nada que era **perfecto**.*

Then they saw it.
A rose.
A **perfect** yellow rose.

Después la vieron.
Una rosa.
*Una rosa amarilla **perfecta**.*

Mama's name is Rosa and she loves flowers. We all knew that it would be the perfect gift for her!

Maria and Carlos raced to the counter to pay for the flower.

El nombre de Mamá es Rosa y a ella le encantan las flores. Todos supimos que sería el perfecto regalo para ella!

Maria y Carlos corrieron al mostrador a pagar por la flor.

Mr. Garcia looked at them sadly.

"I'm sorry," he said. "This rose costs more than you have."

Señor Garcia los miró con lástima.

"Perdón," el dijo. "Esta rosa cuesta mas de lo que ustedes tienen."

Maria and Carlos were terribly disappointed.

Then Maria's face brightened as she said, "Maybe Ricky will help us buy it!"

Carlos smiled up at me. "Will you help us, Ricky?"

Maria y Carlos estaban terriblemente desilusionados.
Entonces la cara de Maria cambio al decir.
  "Posiblemente Ricky nos puede ayuda a comprarla!"
Carlos sonrio y dijo. "Nos ayudas, Ricky?"

I already had a gift for Mama. It was a pen with ink you could see in the dark.

Yo ya había comprado un regalo para Mamá. Era un lapizero con tinta que se podía ver hasta en el oscuro.

Maria reminded me that I still had some **money** left. But I told her that Grandma and I were going to a big fancy store later.

*Maria me recordó que todavía me quedaba **dinero**. Pero le dije que mas tarde yo iba con mi abuelita a una tienda grande y lujosa.*

I wanted to buy Mama a pretty card.
I wanted to buy it with the **money** I had left.

Yo queria comprarle a Mamá una tarjeta bonita.
*Y la iba a comprar con el **dinero** que me sobraba.*

GO

"Don't worry, Ricky," said Carlos with a sigh. "We'll just have to find another **gift** for Aunt Rosa."

Mr. Garcia helped them pick out a yummy sweet bun and a chocolate bar.

*"No te preocupes, Ricky," dijo Carlos suspirando. "Tendremos que encontrar otro **regalo** para tia Rosa."*

El Señor Garcia los ayudo a escojer un rico pan dulce y un chocolate.

I told Maria that Mama was going to love the **gifts**.

But Maria was kind of sad.

*Le dije a Maria que les iba a gustar los **regalos** a Mamá.*

Pero Maria estaba un poco triste.

Then suddenly Maria spotted the most amazing thing. Growing through the cracks of the sidewalk was a pretty, yellow flower. She stopped and pointed, very excited!

"Look," she shouted. "It's a yellow **rose**!"

Derepente Maria vió algo muy increible. Creciendo por las rajaduras de la vereda estaba una flor amarillo bonita. Ella paró y apunto muy exitada.

*"Mira," ella grito. "Es una **rosa** amarilla!"*

I told her it was just a weed.
But she said it was as pretty as a **rose**.
She bent down to pick it.

Le dije que era solo una yerba mala.
*Pero ella dijo que era tan bonita como una **rosa**.*
Se agacho a cojerla.

"Wait," I yelled. "The **flower** will die if you pick it."
Maria stopped and gave a big, sad sigh.
"But maybe it will be okay if you dig it up," I said doubtfully.

"*Espera*," *yo grité.* "*La **flor** morirá si la sacas.*"
Maria paró y dio un suspiro grande y triste .
"*Pero posiblemente estaria bien si la escarbas,*" *le dije con duda.*

Mr. Garcia gave us a cup.
We put the **flower** in the cup.
Then we took it home.

El Señor Garcia nos dió una taza.
*Pusimos la **flor** en la taza.*
Después la llevamos a casa.

We slipped quietly into our apartment, hoping that Mama wouldn't see us. But Grandma told us that Mama was out shopping, and we didn't have to **worry**.

Entramos despacio a nuestro apartamento, con la esperanza que Mamá no nos vea. Pero Abuelita nos dijo que Mamá habia salido de compras, y que no teniamos que **preocuparnos**.

Maria and Carlos did not **worry**.
They had the perfect birthday gift for Mama at last.

*Maria y Carlos no se **preocuparon**.*
Al fin tenían el regalo perfecto para el cumpleaños de Mamá.

Then Carlos noticed the flower looked kind of droopy.
"It just needs water," Maria said confidently. "That's what Mama gives her plants when they look **droopy**."
I wasn't so sure.

*Entonces Carlos se dió cuenta que la flor lucia media **caida**.*
"Solo necesita agua," dijo Maria con confianza. "Eso es lo que Mamá le da a sus plantas cuando lucen caidas."
Yo no estaba tan seguro.

Maria gave the flower some water.
Carlos gave it water too.
But the flower was still **droopy**.

Maria le dio un poco de agua a la flor.
Carlos le dio agua también.
*Pero la flor seguia **caida**.*

"Sometimes Mama feeds her plants," said Maria. "Maybe it needs some **food**."

Carlos agreed with Maria and, before I could stop them, they raced off to the kitchen!

*"A veces Mamá les da de comer a sus plantas," dijo Maria. "Posiblemente necesita **comida**."*

Carlos le dio la razon a Maria y, antes que los podía detener, los dos corrieron a la cocina!

They put some **food** in the cup.
They waited for the flower to look better.
But the flower still looked very droopy.

*Pusieron un poco de **comida** en la taza.*
Esperaban que la flor lucíera mejor.
Pero la flor todavía lucía bien caída.

Carlos was getting discouraged. But not Maria.

Then she said, "Maybe it just misses its home in the sidewalk crack. Maybe we just need to make it feel better."

Carlos se estába desanimando. Pero Maria no.

Después ella dijo, "Posiblemente solo extraña su casa en la rajadura de la vereda y solo necesitamos hacerla sentirse mejor."

Maria gave the flower a big kiss.
Then she and Carlos sang to it.
I smiled as I watched them.

Maria le dio un gran beso a la flor.
Después ella y Carlos le cantaron.
Me sonreí al mirarlos.

Just then **Grandma** came in to say that Mama was home.
"Come on, Ricky," she said. "We can go to the store now and get that pretty card for your mom."

*En ese momento **Abuelita** entro para decirme que Mamá estaba en casa.*
"Vamos, Ricky," me dijo. "Ahora podemos ir a la tienda y comprar la tarjeta para tu mama."

"Okay, **Grandma**," I said.
I started to go.
Then I stopped and looked at Maria and Carlos.

*"Ya voy, **Abuelita**," le conteste.*
Empece a ir.
Entonces me paré y miré a Maria y Carlos.

Maria was carefully wrapping the flower in her favorite blanket while Carlos gently stroked its petals.

Maria estába envolviendo la flor con mucho cuidado en su frazada favorita mientras que Carlos le acaricíaba los pétalos.

They really cared about the flower.
They wanted Mama to have the perfect gift.

De verdad querían a la flor.
Ellos querían que Mamá recibíera el regalo perfecto.

Then I told them, "Don't worry. Your flower will be just fine. Mama always says that her flowers grow so big and strong because of the love she gives them. She says love can work **miracles**."

*Entonces les dije, "No se preocupen, sus flor estará muy bien. Mamá siempre dice que sus flores crecen grandes y fuertes por el amor que les dá. Ella dice que el amor puede hacer **milagros**."*

Maria smiled.

"Then I am going to give this flower all the love in the world—and make a **miracle**!"

Maria sonrió.

*"Entonces yo voy a darle a esta flor todo el amor del mundo—y hare un **milagro**!"*

Grandma and I went down to the bus stop to wait for the bus that would take us to the department store.

The bus came. The bus went.

Grandma and I were still standing at the bus stop.

Abuelita y yo fuímos al paradero para esperar al autobús que nos llevaría a la tienda grande.

El autobús vino. El autobús se fue.

Abuelita y yo todavía estábamos parados en el paradero.

I looked at Grandma and said, "Let's go to Mr. Garcia's market."
Grandma smiled at me.

Yo miré a Abuelita y le dije, "Vamos al mercado del Señor Garcia."
Abuelita sonrió conmigo.

Bright and early the next morning, Carlos came over and ran to Maria's bedroom. Grandma and I followed him.

Maria showed Carlos the flower and exclaimed, "Look! Our flower has become a **beautiful** yellow rose."

Temprano la próxima mañana, Carlos vino y corrió al cuarto de Maria. Abuelita y yo lo seguimos.

*Maria le enseño la flor y exclamó, "Mira! Nuestra flor se a vuelto una rosa amarilla **linda**."*

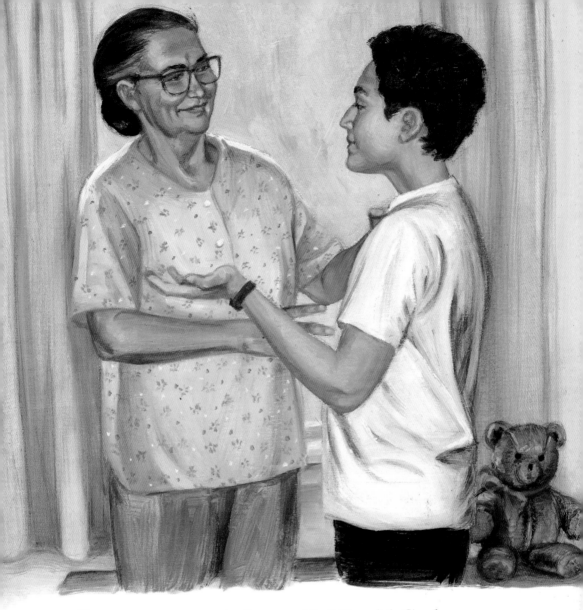

"It really is **beautiful**," said Carlos.
Grandma smiled at me.
"Yes. It really is."

*"De verdad esta **linda**," dijo Carlos.
Abuelita se sonrió conmigo.
"Sí. De verdad si es."*

Mama loved the yellow rose. And she loved the sweet bun, the chocolate bar and the pen with ink you could see in the dark. And she loved the homemade card I gave her.

She opened it and read:

A Mamá le encantó la rosa amarilla. Y le encanto el pan dulce, el chocolate y el lapizero con tinta que se ve hasta en el oscuro. Y le encanto la tarjeta que le hice.

Ella la abrío I leyó:

Love can work miracles.
Like a perfect yellow rose.

El amor puede hacer milagros.
Como una rosa amarilla perfecta.

If you liked
***The Perfect Gift (El Regalo Perfecto),* here are two
other *We Both Read*® Books you are sure to enjoy!**

Ben and Becky are back for another big adventure!
This time they set out to solve the mystery of a
haunted house and find their lost grandfather! The
action is fun and exciting and the reading level is
perfect for the slightly more advanced beginning
reader.

The Wicked Witch has banned birthdays in Munchkin Land! Two Munchkin children, Meezie and Tweeze, are forced to cancel their birthday celebration, but then decide to take matters into their own hands and challenge the Witch's ban. With the help of their friend, Windbag, they just might succeed and rid Munchkin Land of the Wicked Witch forever.

DEMCO